MW00860573

José AND Feliz PLAY FÚTBOL

For Mya, Oliver, Evie, Benny, and Ziggy—SR

For Bitty—SL

To Francisco—without him none of this would be possible—GF

PENGUIN WORKSHOP
An imprint of Penguin Random House LLC, New York

First published simultaneously in paperback and hardcover in the
United States of America by Penguin Workshop, an imprint of
Penguin Random House LLC, New York, 2023

Visit us online at penguinrandomhouse.com.

Library of Congress Cataloging-in-Publication Data is available.

Manufactured in China

ISBN 9780593521205 (hc) 10 9 8 7 6 5 4 3 2 1 TOPL

Design by Jamie Alloy

José and Feliz Play Fútbol

By Susan Rose and Silvia López

Illustrated by Gloria Félix

PENGUIN WORKSHOP

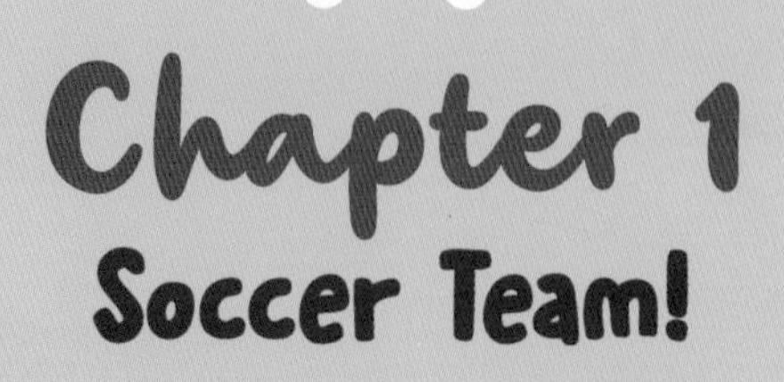

Chapter 1
Soccer Team!

José was very excited.

Yesterday he had been picked for the school soccer team. Finally, he was part of el equipo de fútbol!

Practices would start in a few days.

José wanted to do well.

Today, he planned to practice at home.

He ran up to his house. As always, his dog, Feliz, waited at the window.

José and el perro were best friends.

Feliz jumped up and down behind la ventana. “Woof!” he barked.

José knew what Feliz meant: “Mi mejor amigo is home!”

At José's house, everyone spoke English y español. José had taught Feliz commands in both languages.

"¡Siéntate!" Feliz sat.

"¡Trae!" Feliz fetched.

“¡Quédate!” Feliz stayed.

And by now, el perro understood lots of other words, too.

Chapter 2
A Surprise

José hopped on one foot around the kitchen. He was putting on his soccer shoes.

The cleats made *clickety-clack* sounds around la cocina.

"Funny zapatos!" laughed his little sister, Sofi.

"We have a surprise for you, José," Mami said.

Sofi clapped. "¡Sí, sí, una sorpresa!"

"Look outside," said Papi. "Mira afuera."

José rushed to the backyard with Feliz at his heels.

Wow! There was a soccer goal net and a new ball! And even two big orange cones!

José placed el balón de fútbol on the ground.

Whoosh! **He kicked it toward the net. Feliz went after it like a flash!**

El perro dug his teeth into the ball. He brought it back to José.

"No, Feliz. No lo traigas. We are not playing fetch," José said.

Feliz looked a little confused.

"Never mind. I will practice dribbling instead," José said.

José dribbled el balón around the first cone. He dribbled it around the second cone.

Feliz ran beside him, watching the ball.

When José stopped, Feliz tapped the ball with his nose. He bumped it with his head. He pushed it with his front legs.

Suddenly—*whizz!*—Feliz took off. Tapping the ball con su nariz . . . Bumping it con su cabeza . . . Pushing it con sus patas . . .

He led it fast around the first cone!

¡Rápido!

He led it faster around the second cone!

¡Más rápido!

Finally, he stopped the ball at José's feet.
And sat.

José was amazed!

Feliz could dribble like a real jugador!

Mami, Papi, and Sofi clapped from la ventana in the kitchen. "You and Feliz make a good equipo!" Papi called out.

Chapter 3
Soccer Practice

José sat with the team.

The family watched from the bleachers.
Feliz sat with la familia.

"Woof!" he barked.

Coach Flores talked first about everyday things. Be on time. Wear shin guards. Drink lots of water, mucha agua. Other things, too.

Pass el balón. Work together.

And follow directions. That was very important, muy importante.

Then, he went over the rules of the game. José knew many of las reglas del juego.

He had fútbol books at home. He would read them again.

The kids ran to the field. They dribbled around the cones.

"Toes down! Tap the ball with your shoelaces," the coach called out. "Good job," he told José.

José was glad he had practiced.

"Time to work on kicking," Coach Flores said. *Whoosh!* José kicked el balón toward the net.

Oh no! Feliz jumped from the bleachers.

"¡Vuelve, Feliz! Come back!" Papi shouted.

"Not now!" yelled Mami. "¡Ahora no!"

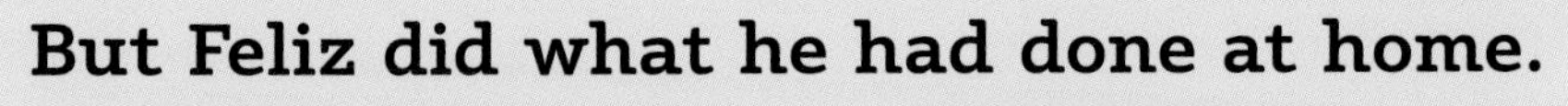

But Feliz did what he had done at home.

He chased the ball and dribbled around the cones. Then he stopped it at José's feet. And sat.

The kids' mouths hung open.

José thought he saw Coach Flores frown.

"I'm sorry . . . ," José mumbled.
"Lo siento . . ."

But the coach let out a big, booming laugh! "That is the best dribbling I ever saw," he said.

The kids laughed, too.

They all ran to Feliz. Todos wanted to pet him.

Slurp! Feliz gave out perro kisses. His whole body wiggled!

"Your dog is so cool!" one kid said.

"Can he be our team mascot?" another kid asked.

Coach Flores rubbed his chin. "Hmmmm," he said. But he was smiling.

Chapter 4
Game Day

José jumped out of bed.

This was it! The first game. ¡El primer partido!

Yesterday, the coach had handed out uniforms. The team colors were red and blue.

He had given José a dog vest, rojo y azul.

"For our mascot," said Coach Flores.

During practices, Feliz sat next to the bench. “Stay. Quédate,” José said.

Feliz did as he was told.

José knew el perro was smart. But what if he forgot?

What if today he ran out and chased el balón?

José petted Feliz. “Remember, boy, quédate,” he told him.

The team ran out to the field. Coach Flores shouted directions.

The kids worked together. They passed to each other. Both equipos were good. The game was tied.

El balón rolled to José. He saw his chance. He kicked and . . .

G-o-o-o-o-o-al!

The whistle sounded.

Game over!

On the field, José's team whooped and high-fived. Their first win!

Papi, Mami, and Sofi cheered from the bleachers.

José looked to the bench. Feliz was jumping up and down. But he had not gone to the field. He had followed directions.

"¡Ven, Feliz! Come!" José shouted.

Feliz rushed out. He ran among the kids. He gave lots of perro kisses.

José bent down and hugged Feliz.

"I'm proud of you. Estoy orgulloso," he said. "You are part of el equipo!"

"Woof!" barked el perro.

José knew what Feliz meant: "And you are mi mejor amigo!"

List of Spanish Words and Phrases

Fútbol: Soccer
El equipo de fútbol: The soccer team
El perro: The dog
La ventana: The window
Mi mejor amigo: My best friend
Y español: And Spanish
¡Siéntate!: Sit!
¡Trae!: Fetch!
¡Quédate!: Stay!
La cocina: The kitchen
Zapatos: Shoes
¡Sí, sí, una sorpresa!: Yes, yes, a surprise!
Mira afuera: Look outside
El balón de fútbol: The soccer ball
No lo traigas: Don't bring it

Con su nariz: With his nose
Con su cabeza: With his head
Con sus patas: With his paws/legs
¡Rápido!: Fast!
¡Más rápido!: Faster!
Jugador: Player
La familia: The family
Mucha agua: Lots of water
Muy importante: Very important
Las reglas del juego: The rules of the game
Vuelve: Come back
¡Ahora no!: Not now!
Lo siento: I'm sorry
Todos: All/everyone
¡El primer partido!: The first game!
Rojo y azul: Red and blue
Ven: Come
Estoy orgulloso: I'm proud (of you)
Jugando: Playing

José y Feliz jugando fútbol